To
Addey

Love you,
Aunt Linda
& Uncle Greg

Little, Brown and Company

Hachette Book Group
1290 Avenue of the Americas, New York, NY 10104
Visit us at lb-kids.com

LB kids is an imprint of Little, Brown and Company.
The LB kids name and logo are trademarks of Hachette Book Group, Inc.

The publisher is not responsible for websites
(or their content) that are not owned by the publisher.

First Edition: July 2015

Library of Congress Control Number: 2015930748

ISBN 978-0-316-26693-2

10 9 8 7 6 5 4 3 2 1

PHX

Printed in the United States of America

minionsmovie.com

MINIONS

Dracula's Last Birthday

By Lucy Rosen
Illustrated by Ed Miller

LITTLE, BROWN & COMPANY
LB kids

Minions have roamed the earth since the beginning of time. Before there was Gru, before there were evil gadgets to invent, before there were super villains who wanted to take over the world…there were Minions.

Ever since the very first Minion crawled out of the ocean and onto dry land, these little yellow creatures have been searching for one thing: the most terrible, wicked, despicable master they could find.

The Minions lived to serve.
They had no trouble tracking
down the biggest, baddest
dinosaur…

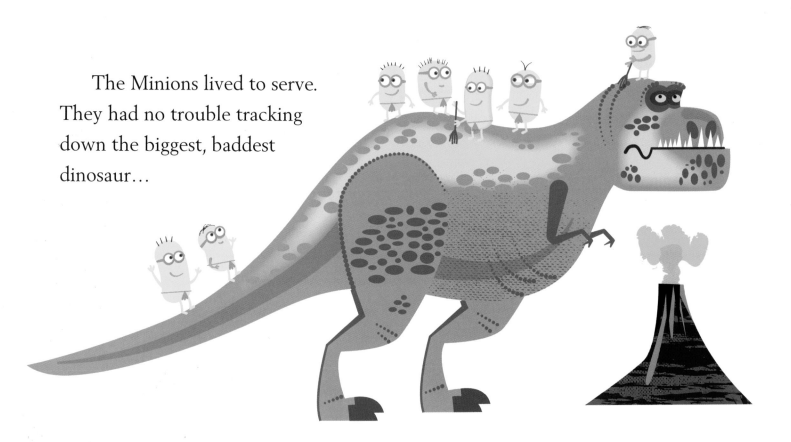

…or helping a wicked pharaoh
erect a pyramid.

OOPS!

But even though they just wanted to help, something always went wrong.

OOPS!

Whenever disaster struck, the Minions kept moving. One day, they came across a dark stone castle. It looked creepy, creaky, and cold. It was perfect! The Minions couldn't wait to meet whoever lived there.

The Minions pushed open the front door and peeked inside. Out of nowhere, bats came flying toward them!

"Oh, la no! Stopa, stopa!" they cried, trying to get away from the bat attack. The Minions tumbled into dusty cobwebs. They jumped into sticky cauldrons. They hid behind heavy, dirty curtains.

When the bats finally left, the Minions came out of their hiding spots and looked around. At the end of the long, dark hallway was a spooky wooden coffin. "Oooooh," they said.

One of the Minions walked up to the coffin. He knocked on the lid. It burst wide open. Dracula was inside!

"Velcome to my castle!" the evil vampire bellowed.

"Si, si, si!" cried the Minions. They couldn't believe it. They had found their new master!

"Big boss! Big boss! Big boss!" they cheered.

BIG BOSS!

The Minions got right to work trying to help Dracula however they could. First, they decided to clean up the castle. Carl and Mike took turns sweeping the cobwebs.

"Me do it," Carl said.

"No, me, me do it," Mike replied.

"Speta, me la do it," Carl insisted.

"Me!" said Mike.

"Me!" said Carl.

Soon enough, the two Minions were tussling
down the hallway. They bounced and rolled and
rumbled all around, until they got tangled up in
an enormous web!

Next, the Minions replaced all of
Dracula's melted candles. One by one,
they removed the old wax. They carefully
polished each candlestick. They gently put
in fresh new candles.

Then they lit them all with a torch.

Finally, at the end of every day, the Minions helped Dracula get ready to go to sleep. They hung up his cape, fluffed his itchy pillow, and reminded him to always brush his fangs before bedtime.

"Scusa, big boss? Floss-floss?" they said.

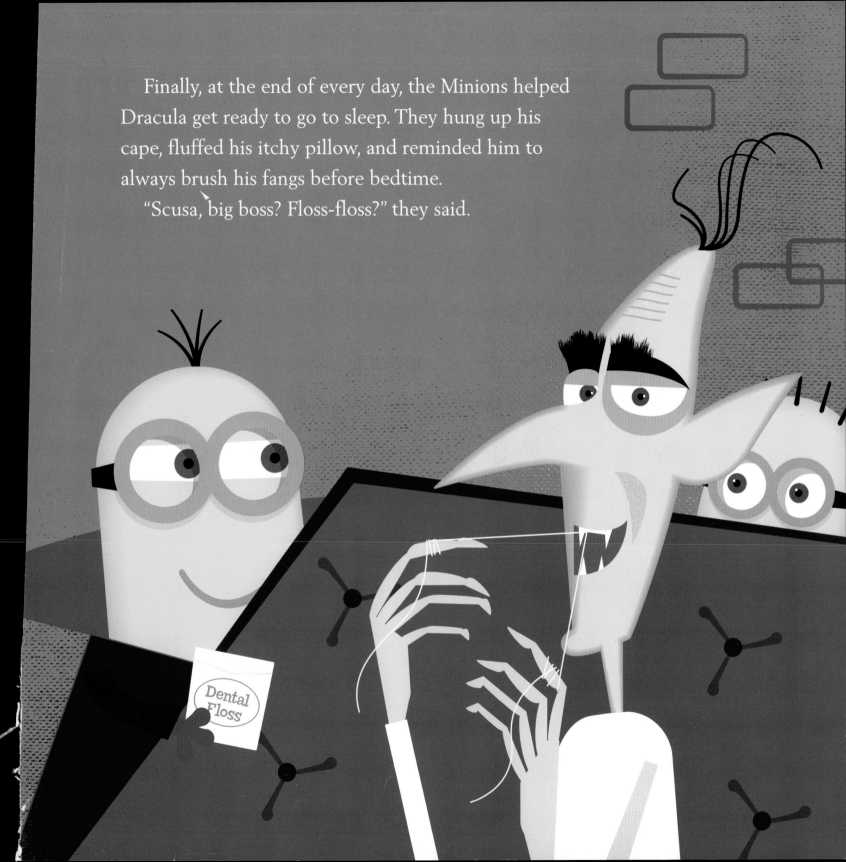

Over time, Dracula came to rely on the
Minions and think of them as his friends. He
even let them in on a secret.

"Tomorrow vill be my three-hundred-und-
fifty-seventh birthday!" he said proudly.

The Minions were excited. They wanted to throw their evil boss an evil party to celebrate his many years of evildoing. But they didn't have much time.

Kevin made a list of all the things they'd need to do: Bake a cake. Make drinks. Find a great gift…

Dave and Paul got started on the cake. They mixed together eggs, flour, strawberries, and sugar. "Yum, yum," they said.

Chuck and Norbert made punch in one of Dracula's cauldrons. They put ice cream and fresh fruit in the juice. Delicious!

Finding the right gift was the hardest part. What does a Minion get for the villain who has it all? The Minions put their heads together until they thought of the perfect present: a portrait of Dracula with all his yellow friends by his side.

They got to work painting their masterpiece.

Happy Birthday

Where Dracula had been sitting, there was now a big pile of ashes. The Minions forgot about the vampire's biggest weakness: sunlight!

"Uh, no," said Stuart, slapping his forehead. "Not again."

Another evil boss,
another Minion accident.
The little yellow creatures
sighed and moved on.

Soon, they found another perfect despicable master in a French captain. At least—that is—until they messed up again.

OOPS!